ROBO-RUNNERS

The Ghost Sea

Books in the **Robo-Runners** series:

ROBO-RUNNERS

The Ghost Sea

by DAMIAN HARVEY

Illustrated by Mark Oliver

Hodder Children's Books

A division of Hachette Children's Books

Hodder Children's Books
A division of Hachette Children's Books
338 Euston Road, London NW1 3BH
An Hachette Livre UK company

To Laura Harvey
with all of my love

The Ghost Sea lies from the northern slopes of
the Mountains of Khan, all the way to the ancient
walled city of Tarka. Great ships used to battle
their way through the waves, delivering cargo and
passengers to ports that lined the coasts. But that
was many years ago.

Now, only the most desperate of travellers
would dare cross this sea, and the only ships
spotted off the coasts belong to pirates and
scavengers. Monsters roam the sea beds, and
plundered wrecks litter the shores and sand dunes.

Towards this desolate sea came four robot
friends, Crank, Al, Grunt and Avatar, travelling in

search of a safe place for old robots.

A place where robots can be free to live their lives in peace.

A place called Robotika.

One minute the four friends had been flying high above the clouds in the *Starship Terrapin* and the next they were dropping through them, trailing smoke and flames from a damaged engine pod.

Avatar pulled as hard as she could on the flight stick but it made no difference. The ship continued dropping at a frightening speed.

"I can't even tell where we are," complained Avatar, looking at the vid-screen. "The clouds are so thick I can't see a thing."

Al, with an anti-grav belt strapped round his waist, was hovering over the navigation screen trying to work out where they were.

"According to this we should be somewhere over the Ghost Sea," he said. "Perhaps we can splash down safely and wait to be picked up."

"Who's going to pick us up?" said Crank. "No one knows we're here. Anyway, this ship's so full of holes that it'll sink as soon as we hit the water."

"I don't think you need to worry about sinking," said Avatar. "Look!"

As the *Starship Terrapin* broke through the clouds the Ghost Sea came into view.

"Where is it?" asked Crank.

"According to the nav-screen it is right there," said Al.

"But where's the water?" said Crank. "I thought seas were supposed to be big and wet."

"Well dis one looks big and dry," said Grunt. "And I fink we is gonna hit it … We is finished."

"We're not finished yet," said Avatar, pulling on the flight stick again. "Give me a hand, Grunt."

Grunt, the biggest and strongest of the four friends, pulled on the flight stick as hard as he could. With a loud crunch, it ripped out of the floor, bringing a trail of smoking wires and sparking contacts along with it.

"Oops," said Grunt. "I don't fink it's supposed to do dat."

"*Now* we're finished," sighed Avatar, looking at the broken flight stick in Grunt's hand.

"What are we going to do?" cried Crank.

Through the vid-screen at the front of the *Starship Terrapin*, the four friends could see the ground rushing towards them as the craft plummeted out of control.

"We is gonna crash," said Grunt, nodding his head.

"I can see that," said Crank. "I meant, what can we do to stop it?"

"We can start by strapping ourselves in," said Avatar, taking a seat and fastening the safety belts over her shoulders.

The ship rattled and shook as it fell through the air – making it difficult to get into a seat and almost impossible to fasten the safety belts – but eventually, Crank, Al and Grunt managed to strap themselves in next to Avatar.

Scamp, the botweiler, a robo-dog that went everywhere with Grunt, tried to crawl beneath one of the seats but was just too big. Instead, he let out a loud whine and lay with his head next to Grunt's feet.

"Right," said Crank. "Now what?"

"This is the easy part," said Avatar. "Now we crash."

The *Starship Terrapin* hit the ground with a joint-shattering crunch and its nose dug into the earth, ploughing a trench in the sea bed. A shower of sand and dried mud flew into the air as it went along.

Inside the ship, smoke filled the air and sparks flew from the control panels and rained down on the four friends. Then the vid-screen on the wall exploded, showering them all with glass.

Scamp, the botweiler, let out a loud metallic howl as the lights blinked out. The control room was plunged into darkness but still the ship sped along, shaking and rattling as it ploughed through the earth, hitting rocks and boulders, before eventually coming to a shuddering halt.

"Well," said Al, unfastening his safety belts, "that could have been worse."

"Worse!" cried Crank. "We've just crash-landed in the middle of a sea that looks like it's been dead for hundreds of years. How could it be worse than that?"

"We could have ended up beneath the water," said Al, fiddling with the control buttons on his anti-grav belt. "Although new robots like me are able to function underwater I do not think the same thing can be said about you."

"He's right," said Avatar. "Things *could* be a lot worse. At least we're still in one piece ... which is more than can be said for the ship."

The *Terrapin* had been a wreck when they had first climbed on board but now it looked even worse. Large dents had appeared in the ship's hull, and light was shining in through many of the cracks and holes that had opened up. A mixture of sand and dirt was falling in through some of the holes and piling up on the control panels.

"Come on," growled Grunt, getting up from his chair without bothering to unfasten the safety straps. "Let's ged out of 'ere."

As Grunt made his way towards the boarding ramp at the back of the ship the safety straps snapped like cotton and his seat crashed to the floor.

"Come on," he said. "What is you waiting for?"

Al was still fiddling with the buttons on his anti-grav belt. He'd tried tapping and hitting them a couple of times but nothing was happening.

"The power cells are dead," said Avatar, examining the belt.

"Oh great," said Al, looking miserably at the anti-grav belt. "It looks as though I am back to running around on my hands. So humiliating for a state of the art robot like me."

Despite a few scratches and having had his legs pulled off by the Tin Man in the recycling plant, Al was still a new robot and never missed a chance to remind his friends that he was fitted with the latest in robot technology.

"Don't worry," said Avatar, joining Grunt by the boarding ramp. "The belt's solar-powered so it'll soon charge itself up again once you've been outside for a while."

"On no!" cried Grunt. "Dare's no power for da boarding ramp ... It's dead ... we is trapped in here."

"No!" cried Crank, falling to his knees and covering his face with his hands.

"Hur, hur hur," laughed Grunt. "Grunt is only teasing."

Grunt pulled the emergency release lever and the boarding ramp fell open. "Ta-da," he said. "Ladies an' gentlemen, welcome to da Ghost Sea."

As the four friends got their first glimpse of the Ghost Sea a huge claw shot in through the open doorway, plucked Grunt from the back of the wrecked *Terrapin* and dragged him out of sight.

As Grunt disappeared, Scamp leaped after him, growling and baring his razor-sharp teeth.

"Grunt!" yelled Avatar, rushing to the open doorway where the big robot had been standing.

Avatar peered down from the ship but there was no sign of Grunt or Scamp anywhere.

"What *was* that?" asked Crank.

"I've no idea," said Avatar. "But whatever it is, it's got Grunt."

"Look," said Al. "There are tracks in the earth. It seems that not *everything* in the Ghost Sea is dead after all."

"Come on," said Avatar. "We'll have to rescue him."

The thought of anything big enough and strong enough to pick Grunt up and carry him away made Crank's circuits shake.

"Don't you think it would be better if we just stayed here?" he asked hopefully. "I'm sure Grunt can take care of himself and we might just get in the way."

"You might be right," said Avatar. "But I still think we should make sure."

From somewhere outside the ship the three friends heard a loud metallic howl.

"That's Scamp," said Avatar. "Come on."

"Er ..." said Crank, scratching at the flaking paint on his head.

"Now what?" said Avatar, impatiently.

"I was just wondering whether that noise was the sound of Scamp attacking something or whether it was something attacking Scamp."

Avatar didn't answer. Instead, she leaped from the open doorway of the *Terrapin* and landed

gracefully in the channel that the wrecked starship
had ploughed into the sea bed.

"Come on!" she yelled. "Jump!"

Crank peered down at Avatar and then stepped
back again, away from the edge. "It's a long way
down," he called.

"You'll be fine," replied Avatar. "It's not as far as
it looks."

"Go on," said Al. "Think of Grunt … Just jump."

"I am thinking of Grunt," said Crank, peering back over the edge. "But I can't help thinking of that big claw as well. I'm just getting myself ready and then I'll … Arghhh!"

Crank dived from the open doorway and landed head first on the ground below.

"He pushed me," cried Crank, glaring up at Al as Avatar helped him to his feet.

"Nonsense," said Al, landing beside him. "I was only helping."

"The next time I need *your* help I'll let you know," shouted Crank.

"When you two have finished arguing," said Avatar, "it's *Grunt* that needs our help."

The three friends clambered up out of the channel and looked for the tracks that Al had spotted earlier.

The mud of the sea bed was cracked and dry with patches of salt lying here and there like frost.

In front of them a sand dune sloped upwards and it was towards this that a trail of deep claw marks led, making it easy to see which way Grunt had been taken.

"Come on!" said Avatar, setting off up the sand dune.

From somewhere ahead of them there came a crunching sound, followed closely by a loud cry.

"That sounded like Grunt," said Al, running as quickly as his hands would carry him. "Hurry, before we are too late."

From the top of the dune, the Ghost Sea could be seen stretching like a desert into the hazy distance. Between long stretches of dried mud other sand dunes rose like rippling waves, and the wrecks of ancient ships lay half buried amongst them ... but the three friends hardly noticed any of it.

At the other side of the dune stood a giant crab with one huge claw snapping and clicking in the air.

In front of it stood Grunt, swinging his fists and ducking and diving out of the way as the crab tried to grab hold of him.

CLACK went the crab's claw as it snapped closed.

Grunt ducked just in time and the deadly claw missed him by a whisker.

"Ouch!" said Crank. "That looked close."

CLACK, CLACK went the claw again, slicing at the air where Grunt had been standing only a second before.

Grunt rolled to one side as the claw swung towards him and then leaped forwards, punching the crab's armoured shell with one huge fist.

TACKA-TACKA-TACKA went the crab's legs on the sun-baked mud as it shuffled back.

The three friends watched as Grunt leaped towards the crab again only to be batted away by its lethal claw.

TACKA-TACKA-TACKA.

As the big robot fell on to his back the crab scuttled forwards, driving its huge claw straight down towards him.

Grunt managed to roll to one side just in time and the claw dug into the hard mud.

"Why doesn't he just run?" asked Crank.

"Look!" said Avatar. "It's Scamp."

Scamp, the botweiler, was pinned to the ground beneath the monster crab's other pincer.

"He is trying to rescue Scamp," said Al.

"Come on," said Avatar, running down the sand dune. "We've got to help."

"Oh great," groaned Crank. "I just knew she was going to say something like that."

Avatar and Al charged down the sloping sand dune towards the giant crab.

"Wait for me,"
shouted Crank,
picking up a
thick piece
of driftwood
and running
after them.

Grunt swung
his fist at the giant
crab again but this time
the crab lashed out with its huge
claw and snapped around Grunt's wrist.

"Arrrghhh!" howled Grunt, as the crab lifted
him off his feet.

Avatar somersaulted high into the air and landed
on top of the monster crab. She raced across its
armoured back and dived along its arm, landing on
top of the huge claw that was holding Grunt.

While Avatar tried to pull the claw open to
release his trapped arm, Grunt bashed it with his

free hand. But the crab wasn't ready to let go just yet.

"Do something," said Al, hopping from hand to hand in front of the crab.

Running down the sand dune towards them, Crank gripped the thick piece of driftwood as tightly as he could and raised it above his head. He knew it was up to him to save his friends, but he had no idea what an old robot like him could do against the giant crab.

"Yaaaaaa!" yelled Crank and charged at the crab. *TACKA-TACKA-TACKA.*

The crab turned to face Crank and swung its huge claw towards him, but the weight of Grunt and Avatar was too much and the claw dropped to the ground with Grunt beneath it.

With the driftwood still above his head, Crank dodged to one side, avoiding the claw, and kept on running.

But then it happened …

Crank tripped up.

Not long after they'd first met, Al had pulled Crank's leg off. Al insisted it had been an accident and repaired the leg while they were in the recycling plant. But unfortunately, he'd attached Crank's leg the wrong way round.

For most of the time, having one leg the wrong way round didn't bother Crank, but every now and then he would trip over his own feet, and that's what happened now.

"Waaaaaaa!" he yelled, flying through the air and letting go of the thick piece of driftwood.

As Crank landed in a heap on the dried mud of the sea bed, the piece of wood flew through the air and hit the crab right between the eyes.

Letting out a high-pitched screech, the crab started running backwards, lifting both claws to protect itself.

When it moved back, the crab's huge claw opened and Grunt fell to the floor. Scamp, freed from beneath the other claw, was up and beside his friend in an instant, growling and baring his teeth at the crab.

Avatar, still holding on to its arm, jumped away from the creature and rolled gracefully across the floor towards Crank.

"Great shot," she said, getting to her feet. "That was amazing."

Crank looked up, not quite sure what had happened, and saw Avatar smiling at him.

"Erm … it was nothing really," said Crank. "Just my lightning reflexes, I suppose. Has it gone?"

"It's going," said Avatar. "I think Al has gone to make sure."

Al had picked the
piece of driftwood
up from the
floor and
was waving
it around
in the air.

"Go on,"
he shouted.
"Shoo! Leave us alone."

The crab clacked its pincers together but took a
few more steps back, away from the four friends.

TACKA-TACKA-TACKA went its claws on the
hard mud as it scuttled out of sight into a dip in
the dried sea bed.

"Yes!" shouted Al, triumphantly waving the stick
in the air again as he hopped back to join his
friends. "It will not mess with us again."

Avatar and Crank had gathered round Grunt,
who was still sitting on the floor.

"I fink it's broken," said Grunt, shaking his head sadly and examining the hand that had been gripped in the giant crab's pincer. "It don't look right."

"Do not worry," said Al. "I am programmed to carry out many tasks including simple robot repairs. I am sure I can fix your hand."

"Is dat right?" said Grunt.

"Oh yes," said Crank. "He did a great job of fixing my leg."

"Dat's all right den," said Grunt.

"I was being sarcastic," said Crank. "He put my leg on the wrong way round."

"Looks all right to me," said Grunt. "Here, take a look at my hand."

Grunt held his hand up and the others stared at it in silence for a moment. Grunt had huge strong hands that had been perfect for ripping metal apart when he'd worked in the junk yard, but the one he was holding up now hardly even looked like a hand any more.

"Ouch!" said Crank, wincing. "It looks like a train's run over it."

"I can't feel da fingers no more," said Grunt sadly.

Al put the big piece of driftwood down and looked closely at Grunt's hand. "It is probably not as bad as it looks," he said. "Can you move it?"

Grunt held his arm out and frowned as he concentrated on trying to move his hand.

There was a squeak, a soft grinding noise and a small puff of white smoke came from his wrist joint.

"It don't normally do dat," said Grunt. Then the mangled hand fell to the floor with a CLUNK.

Scamp let out a whine and picked the hand up between his teeth.

"Good boy, Scamp," said Grunt, taking the hand out of the botweiler's mouth and patting him on the head with it.

"Oh dear," said Al. "It might have been as bad as it looked after all."

"Don't worry," said Avatar. "I'm sure we will find another hand for you."

"Yeah," said Grunt. "Dat would be really handy, hur, hur, hur."

Crank wasn't sure whether they *would* be able to find another hand for Grunt. After all, they still hadn't managed to find any new legs for Al, but perhaps something would turn up as they carried on searching for Robotika.

"Come on," he said. "Let's get going."

TACKA-TACKA-TACKA.

"What was that?" asked Avatar.

"I said let's get—"

"No!" interrupted Avatar. "That noise."

"It is that giant crab again," said Al. "But do

not worry. I will see it off."

Picking up the big piece of driftwood again, Al hopped off towards the dip in the sea bed where the giant crab had disappeared.

Al had only gone a short distance when he stopped and dropped the piece of wood.

"Run!" he shouted.

The three friends looked round to see Al dashing towards them on his hands with the giant crab close behind him waving its pincers in the air.

"Dis isn't da time for runnin' away," growled Grunt. "I has had enough. Dis is da time for bashing.'"

Al raced past Grunt as fast as his hands would carry him. "Run!" he shouted. "There are more of them."

"More of dem?" said Grunt. "Bring dem on. Dey will remember da day dey messed wiv Grunt."

As Grunt got close to the giant crab he clenched his teeth and gripped the remains of his broken hand.

"You is in for such a bashin'," said Grunt. "You is not gonna know what has hit y—"

Then he stopped.

From the dip in the sea bed, Grunt could see lots of claws waving in the air. As he watched, more giant crabs came into view. Some of them were even bigger than the one in front of him.

Grunt turned and ran.

"What is it?" asked Avatar.

"I has changed my mind," shouted Grunt. "Dis *is* da time for runnin' after all."

Avatar and Crank took one look at the giant crabs and ran after Al and Grunt.

TACKA-TACKA, TACKA-TACKA went the crabs.

"Dis doesn't look good," shouted Grunt, running beside Al.

"Over the sand dunes," shouted Avatar. "I'm sure I saw an old ship close by. Perhaps we can hide in there."

The four friends ran up the sloping side of the next sand dune and sure enough, from the top they could see the remains of an old ship. Battered and rusted, it was lying in the sand at the bottom of the next row of dunes. If they could reach it in time they might be able to hide from the giant crabs. But between where they stood and the ship itself was a wide stretch of hard, dry sea bed.

The four friends raced down the side of the sand dune, slipping and sliding as they went. Scamp reached the sun-baked sea bed first and set off at a run towards the wrecked ship in the distance.

"Clever boy, Scamp," said Grunt. "'E knows where we is going."

"Anywhere away from those crabs sounds good to me," said Crank.

TACKA-TACKA, TACKA-TACKA.

The first of the crabs had already made it down the sand dune and was chasing them across the flat sea bed.

"It's gaining on us," cried Avatar. "Faster!"

"We'll never make it," said Crank. "It's too far."

Grunt stopped running and turned round to face the first crab.

"What are you doing?" asked Al, hopping past on one hand as he poked at the buttons on his anti-grav belt with the other.

"Jus' keep goin'," said Grunt. "I is gonna slow dis crab down a bit."

TACKA-TACKA-TACKA.

Seeing that Grunt had stopped running, the crab slowed down and raised its huge claw.

CLACK, CLACK went the claw, snapping at the air in front of Grunt.

"Oh yes," growled Grunt. "You'd like to get your claws on me again, wouldn't you."

TACKA-TACKA-TACKA, CLACK, CLACK.

The giant crab scuttled towards Grunt, raising its huge claw again, but Grunt was ready for it.

Clenching his fingers around the crushed remains of his hand, Grunt pulled his arm back and threw.

CLACK, CLACK,

THUB.

The broken hand hit the crab just beneath its thick armoured shell and sent it scuttling back towards the sand dunes with a loud screech of pain.

Grunt didn't wait to see what it would do next, because the rest of the crab army was already coming over the top of the dune. He turned and ran.

Crank, Al and Avatar had made it halfway to the next row of sand dunes when Grunt finally caught up with them.

"Dat slowed it down a bit," said Grunt. "I knew dat broken hand would come in handy for somefink. Hur, hur, hur."

"I do not think this is the time for joking," said Al. "If we do not reach that wreck the rest of the crabs will catch up with us."

TACKA-TACKA, TACKA-TACKA.

"They've made it down the sand dune already," said Crank, looking back. "And they can run much faster on the flat sea bed."

"We're almost there," said Avatar. "Keep going."

Now that they were getting closer they could see the wrecked ship was much bigger than it had first appeared. Half buried in the dunes, the ship stood upright and looked as though it was riding the waves instead of sitting stranded on the dry sand.

The battered hull was full of holes and red with rust. The glass was missing from the windows, making them look like dark, empty eye sockets. Cabin walls and decks, once painted brilliant white, were now caked with dust and grime.

"I've got a bad feeling about that ship," said Crank. "It doesn't look very friendly."

"You can wait for da crabs if you like," said Grunt. "But I *know* dey isn't friendly."

TACKA-TACKA, CLACK, CLACK went the crabs' claws as they got closer to the four friends.

"On second thoughts," said Crank, jumping over a small crater in the dried sea bed, "that ship is starting to look very nice indeed."

"I fink it looks beautiful," said Grunt, leaping over another crater.

As they ran, the four friends found themselves leaping and jumping over more and more holes and craters as they tried to get away from the army of crabs.

TACKA-TACKA-TACKA went the crabs as they scuttled across the sun-baked mud.

CLACK, CLACK, CLACK went their lethal claws as they got closer and closer to the four friends.

"That one nearly had me," cried Al, stumbling over one of the craters.

"I think we should—"

BOOM.

The rest of Crank's words were drowned out by a loud bang from the ship in front of them.

Something whistled through the air above Crank's head and landed behind them with a *THUD* that shook the ground. Dried mud and sand flew into the air, scattering giant crabs in every direction.

"It's firing at us," cried Crank, diving head first into one of the craters.

"No it's not," said Avatar, as another loud boom sounded out from the ship. "It's firing at the crabs."

The ground beneath their feet shook again

and a second shower of mud flew into the air, scattering more crabs.

TACKA-TACKA, TACKA-TACKA went the crabs as they clambered over each other trying to get away.

"Come on," shouted Avatar above the noise. "Let's go while the crabs are busy."

As they ran across the final stretch of sea bed there was one more loud boom from the ship in front of them and then everything fell silent. By the time the four friends had reached the sand dunes where the ship was lying, even the sound of the crabs had faded away.

"HELLO!" called Avatar, looking up at the ship.

There was no answer so Grunt hammered on the rusting hull with his huge fist.

"OI!" shouted Grunt. "IS DERE ANYBODY HOME?"

When the echoing sound of Grunt's knocking finally faded away a robot with a ragged piece of

material on
its head
peered over
the ship's
railings high
above.

"What do you want?"
asked the robot angrily.

"We want to come aboard," said Crank. "Our ship's crashed and we need—"

"Certainly not," interrupted the robot, and disappeared from view.

The four friends looked at each other in disbelief for a moment, then Grunt shook his head and stepped in through one of the big holes in the side of the ship.

"Well I'm not waiting out here for doze crabs to come back," said Grunt, disappearing into the darkness of the wrecked ship.

Scamp jumped through the hole behind Grunt

and the other three friends clambered in after him.

"Be careful," said Avatar, stepping over a hole in the floor. "This thing looks ready to fall apart at any moment."

The four friends made their way through a maze of darkened rooms and narrow corridors. They squeezed through hatches and climbed rattling staircases.

"We might have been safer fighting the crabs," said Al. A handrail he'd been holding had fallen away from the wall, showering him in rust.

"I fink we is at da top now," said Grunt as he pulled open a hatch and daylight flooded in.

Stepping outside, the four friends found themselves on the main deck of the wrecked ship.

"I'm glad we're out of there," said Crank. "That place was giving me the creeps."

"DON'T MOVE!" yelled a voice from behind them. "UNLESS YOU STOWAWAYS WANT PINNING TO THE DECK."

Crank, Al, Avatar and Grunt froze at the sound of the voice. None of them dared to move.

"That's more like it," said the voice from behind them. "Now all of you stand perfectly still while I take a good look at you."

As they stood there, a figure slowly walked round and inspected them. It was the robot they'd seen looking down from the top of the ship. The one that wasn't going to let them come aboard.

It was one of the oldest robots Crank had ever seen. Its face had been made to look like a human, or softie as the robots called them. It was even wearing a hat and jacket, though most of the material had rotted away over the years. There were holes in the jacket, and the hat – once smart – looked like a tatty piece of material stuck to its head.

In its hands, the robot was holding some sort of huge weapon. Crank had never seen anything like it before but could still tell it was a weapon. The vicious-looking spearhead sticking out from the end made it obvious. From the back of the spearhead ran a length of rope which was coiled over the robot's shoulder and tied off around its waist.

"Just as I thought," said the robot, glaring and waving the weapon at them. "Stowaways!"

"Stowaways?" said Avatar. "We're not stowaways."

"That's right," said the robot with a huge grin. "Welcome aboard the *Manatee*, Captain Stark at your service."

Captain Stark dropped the weapon he was holding, saluted, then bowed deeply to the four friends.

There was a clatter as the weapon hit the floor, then a clunk, and a loud *THUB*.

Something whooshed over Al's head and from behind them came a loud bang. The four friends turned to find that a huge metal spear had buried itself in the cabin wall.

Al stared wide-eyed at the spear. The rope attached to it ran back above his head to the coil over the captain's shoulder. If he'd still had his legs, Al would now be skewered to the wall.

"Sorry about that," said Captain Stark, bustling

past the four friends as he wound up the rope.

"What is that thing?" asked Al.

"This, my boy," said the old robot as he tugged at the arrow, "is a harpoon. I use it when pirates come."

"Pirates?" said Crank, looking around nervously. "What pirates?"

Captain Stark ignored him and kept tugging at the harpoon, but it wouldn't budge.

Grunt stepped back and helped him. There was

a screech of metal on metal, then the harpoon came free, leaving a jagged hole in the cabin wall where it had been.

"Ah, there you are," said Captain Stark, taking the harpoon from Grunt. "Keep your eyes open. I think we might have stowaways on board."

"What?" said Grunt, looking puzzled.

The old robot ignored him and loaded the big harpoon back into its launcher. When he'd finished he looked up at the four friends and stepped back in surprise.

"Welcome aboard the *Manatee*," said the old robot. "Captain Stark at your service."

There was a crash as Captain Stark dropped the harpoon again, saluted, and bowed deeply to the four friends.

Crank, Al, Avatar and Grunt dived out of the way but this time the weapon didn't go off.

"Captain Stark raving mad if you ask me," said Crank, giving the captain a worried look.

"I fink you might be right," said Grunt.

"Old robots get like that sometimes," said Avatar. "I'm sure he's not dangerous though."

"NOT DANGEROUS!" cried Al. "Captain Stark raving there nearly pinned me to the wall."

"Don't be too hard on him," said Avatar. "He's probably been here a long time."

The old robot was looking at them with a friendly smile on his face. "Welcome aboard the *Manatee*," he said again. "Captain Stark at your service."

"Where's the rest of the crew?" asked Avatar, smiling kindly at the captain.

The old robot jerked slightly as though seeing Avatar for the first time. "Captain and crew will be back any minute," he said with certainty. "Gone ashore for spare parts they have. As soon as they're back the engine will be fixed in no time and we'll be off this sandbank with the next tide."

"I thought you said *you* were the captain?" said Crank.

"Acting captain," said the old robot, saluting and bowing deeply. "I'm sure the real captain will be back any time now."

"Regulations state that a robot can only be *second* in command of an active ship," whispered Avatar. "Only a *softie* can be a real captain. They must have left him in charge when they left."

"Well I don't fink dis ship has been active for a very long time," said Grunt, looking round at the rusted decks.

"How long have the others been gone?" asked Crank.

"Captain and crew have been gone for 89 years, three months, two days, nine hours, six minutes and 22 seconds," said Stark.

The four friends looked at each other and Crank shook his head.

"I wonder if everyone else left before he went mad or after?" he said. "I know he makes me want to leave."

"Don't be mean," said Avatar. "Can you imagine what it would be like to be left on this ship all on your own?"

"Yes," said Crank. "And it'd be safer than being left with Captain Stark raving mad and his harpoon gun."

"Well if it wasn't for Captain Stark those crabs would have got us," said Avatar.

At the mention of the word crabs, Stark jumped and ran to the ship's rail. "Crabs!" he shouted. "Man the cannon."

There was a loud *BOOM* which shook the whole ship and a metal ball flew out over the dried sea bed, kicking up dust

and leaving a big crater where it landed.

Avatar ran to join the old robot who was busily reloading the cannon that had been fastened to the ship's deck.

"There you are," cried Captain Stark. "Get this loaded and fire on my command."

"It's all right, captain," said Avatar reassuringly.

"They've gone. The crabs have gone. You saved us from them."

"Good," said the old robot. "Welcome aboard the *Manatee*. I'm—"

"The crabs might have gone," interrupted Al. "But something else is coming. Look!"

6

Looking to the north, across the Ghost Sea, the robots could just make out a large shape in the distance.

"What is it?" asked Crank.

"I can't tell," said Avatar. "It's too far away."

"Fortunately, I was fitted with the latest SPX3 visual sensors," said Al. "They are top of the range robotic eyes."

"Well!" said Grunt. "What is it den?"

Al frowned for a moment as he peered into the distance. "Yes," he said, nodding his head. "That is what I thought."

"JUST TELL US WHAT IT IS," yelled Crank.

"There is no need to shout," said Al. "As well as the latest visual sensors I am also fitted with ultra-hi-tech-specification-audio-receptors."

"What?" said Grunt, frowning.

"He's got ears," sighed Crank.

"It is quite clear to me," said Al, nodding his head, "that the thing in the distance is something quite large."

Crank closed his eyes and counted to ten. "Is that it?" he asked, as calmly as he could.

"Oh no," said Al. "I can also see that whatever it is, it is getting closer."

"Can't you tell *what* it is?" asked Avatar.

"Oh no!" said Al. "It is much too far away for that."

"Well it's gettin' closer very quickly," said Grunt. "And it looks like a ship to me."

"Nonsense," said Crank. "In case you hadn't noticed, there's no sea for the ships to sail in."

"Well you can tell dem dat when dey gets here,"

said Grunt. "And you won't 'ave long to wait."

Looking back across the dried mud of the Ghost Sea, Crank could see what Grunt meant. The thing in the distance *was* getting closer. And quickly too.

"It's a ship," said Crank. "And it's got sails."

"PIRATES!" cried Captain Stark. "MAN THE CANNONS ..."

"Are you sure they're pirates?" asked Avatar.

"Of course," said the old robot. "Who else would dare sail the Ghost Sea in a ship like that?"

"Well I don't really know," said Avatar. "We've never been here before."

"But surely you've heard of Silas Quench," said Stark. "The captain of the *Narwhal* and its crew of loathsome pirates."

"No," said Avatar, shaking her head. "I can't say that I have."

"Well we is gonna meet dem any minute now," said Grunt.

The *Narwhal* was getting closer by the second and the four friends could see it quite clearly.

Unlike the *Manatee*, which was an ancient wreck of rusted metal, the *Narwhal* was made of wood and appeared to be in good condition. Huge sails billowed out from two tall masts that stood on deck, driving the ship along on huge wheels that rolled across the sun-baked sea bed.

On the deck of the *Narwhal*, Crank could see a crowd of figures waving an assortment of weapons in the air. Riding at the front of the ship, like a ghastly figurehead, was the most terrible-looking robot Crank had ever seen.

Its head had a row of spikes running along its centre and its mouth was fixed with an evil grin. Its deeply set eyes burned in the darkness of its face – one red and one yellow.

Crank shuddered at the sight of the approaching ship and the robot at its head made his joints rattle with fear.

"What are we going to do?" he asked.

"Do?" said Stark. "There's nothing we can do. The *Narwhal* and its crew have been sailing the Ghost Sea for as long as anyone can remember. They wreck every ship they come across. They steal the cargo and then kill everyone on board."

"Well, they will have trouble wrecking *this* ship," said Al, looking round at the rusty old wreck.

"Indeed," agreed Stark. "This is a fine ship — but they will take any robots they find on board and make them slaves."

"You've got to stop them," said Avatar. "Use your harpoon."

"Don't you worry," said Stark, gripping the big harpoon gun in his hands. "They've never caught old Stark yet."

As the *Narwhal* and its pirate crew came closer, Stark raised the harpoon gun to his shoulder.

"What's he doing?" asked Crank. "He'll never hit them from here."

"I dunno," said Grunt, shrugging his shoulders. "He ain't even facin' da right way."

"No!" cried Avatar. "He's going to—"

But it was too late. Stark had already pulled the trigger.

With a loud *THUB*, the metal spear shot out over the sand dunes, trailing the length of rope behind it.

"Acting Captain Stark at your service," said the old robot, saluting and bowing deeply to the four friends. "Welcome aboard the *Manatee*."

"I said he was mad," said Crank.

Then the rope around Stark's waist pulled tight and the old robot was yanked off his feet by the harpoon.

The four friends watched in amazement as Stark was pulled from the deck of the *Manatee* and flew out over the sand dunes at the back of the ship.

As the old robot disappeared from sight there was a loud bang from the *Narwhal*.

"They're firing at us," cried Avatar.

The four friends dived to the floor as something big and heavy whistled through the air above their heads.

"Perhaps old Stark was not so mad after all," said Al.

"I think you're right," agreed Crank.

Another loud bang sounded from the *Narwhal*
and a huge ball crashed on to the deck, punching
a hole in the rusty metal. A loud cheer went up
from its crew and a voice cried out above it all.

"Prepare for boarding, you rusty dogs."

Crank knew straight away who that voice
would belong to. It could only be one person.
Only one person would have a voice like that
and only one person would call his crew *rusty dogs*.

The big robot he'd seen riding at the front of the ship.

"Come on," said Crank. "We've got to get out of here."

The four friends got to their feet and looked around, but the pirate ship was already upon them.

Huge anchors had been thrown from the back of the *Narwhal* and Crank could see them dinging into the sand and mud, bringing the ship to a halt.

As soon as it stopped there was a blur of movement in the air and two dark shapes leaped across the gap between the ships.

"I'll teach dem to come aboard wivout askin'," said Grunt, stepping forward to meet the pirates.

Grunt was in the middle of the deck with his giant fist ready to punch when the two invaders landed in front of him, snarling and gnashing their rusty teeth.

"Oh! I see," said Crank. "That's what he meant by rusty dogs."

"Botweilers!" cried Grunt, stepping back as the two robo-dogs snarled at him. "Ged 'em, Scamp."

Scamp was much bigger than the two rusty botweilers that had landed on the ship's deck and Crank and Al had both seen what the robo-dog could do in a fight. The pirate dogs wouldn't stand a chance.

Scamp jumped between Grunt and the two botweilers, baring his teeth and snarling.

"Good boy, Scamp," said Grunt. "You show dem pieces of junk what a *real* robo-dog can do."

As Scamp lowered his head, a deep growl came from between his razor-sharp teeth.

The two old robo-dogs leaped into the air and attacked at the same time. Mouths open, showing rusted, crooked teeth that would tear through metal with a single bite, they both let out a terrible snarl.

"Look out!" cried Crank.

"Don't you worry," said Grunt, nodding his head.

"Scamp can handle dese two buckets of bolts wiv his eyes closed."

The two rusty botweilers snapped their jaws together as they dropped down on Scamp – one going for his head and the other for his neck. The robo-dogs expected to destroy him in one quick go, but their jaws snapped together harmlessly in thin air.

Scamp easily stepped away from the two attacking dogs and watched with interest as they crashed to the floor, snapping their jaws on the deck in front of him.

Then he attacked.

One huge metal paw smashed into the side of the first botweiler's head, sending it spinning across the deck of the *Manatee* where it collided with a cabin wall.

When the second dog lifted its head, Scamp grabbed it in his jaws and tossed it high into the air like a toy.

"Good boy, Scamp," said Grunt. "Dat will teach doze pirates to mess wiv us."

The rusty botweiler fell to the deck of the ship with a clatter and Scamp pounced into the air, intending to come crashing down on top of it to finish the old robo-dog off.

"Smash it!" yelled Crank excitedly.

But before Scamp landed, there was a loud *CRACK* from the pirate's ship, a blur of movement, and the big botweiler was snatched from the air as a heavy net wrapped itself around his legs and body.

Scamp fell to the floor, growling, snarling

and snapping at the net that was pinning him down, but his teeth grated and slid harmlessly on the metal.

"Even *your* mutt won't bite through that net," cackled a small robot as it swung on to the deck of the *Manatee* and landed beside one of the old botweilers.

"You'd better let 'im go," growled Grunt, stepping towards the robot with his hand clenched into a huge fist. "Or I'm gonna flatten you into the floor like a tin can."

"I'm Springer," sneered the little robot as it clipped a metal cable on to the net that held Scamp. "And only Captain Quench tells me what to do."

The metal cable pulled tight and the big botweiler was hoisted high into the air and back across to the other ship.

Grunt made a dive for the net that held Scamp, but missed and landed flat on the deck between the cackling robot and one of the old botweilers.

The old robo-dog got to its feet and snarled at Grunt, baring its jagged teeth in a terrible grin, and the little robot let out another cackling laugh.

"Looks like you're in trouble now," said Springer.

As the old botweiler came towards him, Grunt grabbed Springer by the leg and swung him at the old botweiler.

"Aarghhh!" squealed Springer as he whizzed through the air and smashed into the side of the robo-dog's head.

Grunt quickly got to his feet, still gripping Springer by the leg, and jumped backwards as the dog came towards him again.

Springer had managed to grab a metal bar from the deck of the ship and he started to hammer it against Grunt's leg. "Get off me," he yelled.

Grunt ignored the little robot and swung him once again at the snarling botweiler like a club.

The botweiler snapped its jaws and Springer let

out another scream, this time hitting the old robo-dog with the metal bar.

"Dat's better, Springer," said Grunt. "You whack dat bad dog."

Stepping away from the robo-dog as it came in for another attack, Grunt heard a snarl from behind him. The second robo-dog was back on its feet and walking towards Crank, Avatar and Al, snapping its jaws.

Crank and the others had already spotted the dog coming towards them. One of its eyes were hanging loose from when Scamp had bashed it earlier. The eye turned this way and that with a life of its own and Crank couldn't stop staring at it. Somehow, the robo-dog's damaged eye seemed even scarier than its teeth.

"What are we going to do?" asked Crank, still backing away from the botweiler.

"Without Scamp, there's not much we can do," said Avatar. "There's too many pirates and we'll never get past these botweilers without him."

As she spoke, more of the robot pirates swung across from the other ship and landed on the deck of the *Manatee*. With an assortment of old weapons in their hands, the band of pirates advanced on the four friends.

Grunt, Crank, Al and Avatar had gone as far as they could and were now standing with their backs against the railings at the far side of the wrecked ship.

"I fink we is gonna have to abandon ship," said Grunt, and swung the little robot round above his head before finally letting it go.

With a loud squeal, Springer flew through the air and smashed into the band of robot pirates, sending some of them crashing to the floor like skittles.

"Now!" yelled Grunt.

As the robot pirates staggered around, the four friends turned and gripped the handrails, ready to jump over the side of the ship.

"I don't think you want to do that," said a voice behind them.

Looking up at them from the ground below were the two old robo-dogs. They'd already jumped over the side and were waiting for them with jaws wide open, showing their jagged, rusty teeth.

"Pretty fast for a couple of old dogs, aren't they," said the voice. "Not as fast as yours of course. But there's nothing he can do to help you. He seems to be all tied up at the moment."

The voice behind them sent a shiver through Crank and he knew who it was without looking.

With the two old botweilers waiting on the ground below, there was no escape that way. The friends would be lucky to get fifty paces from the ship before the robo-dogs tore them apart.

Crank let go of the ship's rail, slowly turned around, and found himself staring straight into the burning eyes of the robot he'd seen riding at the front of the pirate ship.

Up close, the robot's eyes seemed to burn even brighter and it looked more terrible and more frightening than when he'd first caught sight of it.

"Hello, Gore," said Avatar. "I'd heard *you'd* been recycled."

The big robot turned its terrible gaze on Avatar and smiled.

"*Recycled?*" said Gore. "You know me better than that, Avatar. No one *ever* gets Gore – Gore gets them."

"Gore?" said Crank, looking puzzled. "*I* thought you were Silas Quench – captain of the *Narwhal* and its crew of loathsome pirates?"

"It's nice to see you've heard of us," said Gore, smiling wickedly. "But *I'm* not Silas Quench. The captain is a softie, the cruellest softie to ever walk the planet."

"A softie?" cried Crank. "Silas Quench is a softie?"

"Of course," said Gore. "You don't think a bunch of fine robots like this would let another robot order them around, do you?"

"That's right," shouted one of the robot pirates, waving a rusty sword in the air. "We'd tear it apart."

"We'd crush its joints," shouted another.

"We'd feed it to the crabs," said a third.

"And remember," said Al, "regulations state that a robot can only be *second* in command of an active ship. A robot could *never* be the *real* captain."

Gore's eyes flashed with anger at this and he grabbed Al by the neck and lifted him into the air.

"Well aren't you the clever one," snarled Gore. "I should destroy you *now*."

"Put him down, Gore," said Avatar. "I'm sure you don't need to destroy a small, defenceless robot to show your crew how tough you are."

Springer, the small robot that Grunt had been using to bash the old botweiler, sniggered at this and Gore's eyes flashed with anger once again.

For a moment, Crank was sure Gore was going to destroy Al right there, but instead, he threw him across the deck of the *Manatee* where he was grabbed by a couple of the other robot pirates.

"Keep hold of that piece of junk," roared Gore as he stomped back across the deck towards the *Narwhal*. "And set sail for the nest."

As Al was carried away by two robot pirates, Gore looked back at the other three friends.

"Bring them to the ship and lash them to the mast," snarled Gore. "I'll see what *the captain* wants to do with them. But keep your eye on that one," he added, pointing at Avatar. "She can be tricky."

"What did he mean by that?" asked Crank.

"I've no idea," said Avatar, suddenly finding something interesting to look at on her foot.

"And how do you two know each other?" continued Crank. "You didn't say anything about it before."

"Why would I?" said Avatar. "I thought Gore

had been crushed long ago. Anyway, it's a long story and I really don't think we've got time for it now."

While they spoke, a wooden plank was laid between the two ships and the three friends were bundled on to the *Narwhal* by the robot pirates.

As soon as the last of the robots was aboard, the anchors were dragged from the ground and the *Narwhal* set off across the sun-baked mud of the Ghost Sea.

On the ship, Al was being guarded by one of the old botweilers but there was nothing Crank, Grunt or Avatar could do to help him as they were pushed past and tied to the mast.

Suddenly, Grunt let out a loud groan.

"What is it?" asked Avatar.

"It's Scamp," said Grunt, looking up towards the top of the mast where a bundle of netting swung gently in the breeze. "Da poor fing will be terrified. He don't like heights."

"Oh yes," said Crank. "It's so much better for us being tied up down here, isn't it."

"Don't worry," said Avatar, "we'll get him down as soon as we can, *and* we'll rescue Al."

"In case you hadn't noticed," said Crank, "someone will have to rescue us first."

"I'll think of something," said Avatar.

"Perhaps you could ask your friend to loosen da ropes," suggested Grunt.

"Gore is *not* my friend," snapped Avatar. "He's—"

But Avatar didn't have a chance to say anything else. The door to the captain's cabin burst open and Gore stepped out. "Good news," he cried, grinning at the friends. "The captain says you can work in the engine room."

"Well isn't that nice," said Avatar. "But we really don't want to be any bother so if you'll just untie us we'll be on our way."

"Nonsense!" cried Gore. "It's no trouble at all. In fact … he insists."

"Yes," said Avatar. "I thought he might."

"SPRINGER, BUZZSAW, GRUBSCREW," roared Gore, and three robots stepped forwards. "Prepare the plank."

The robots with Springer were much bigger than him and one of them had a round saw-blade at the end of its arm. Crank guessed that must be Buzzsaw. Together, the three robots pushed a long plank over the edge of the ship so that it poked out like a diving board.

"We're near the nest, Gore," announced Buzzsaw.

"Very good," said Gore. "Drop the anchors."

As the anchors dug into the ground and brought the *Narwhal* to a halt, the four friends looked at each other.

"Nest!" said Crank. "What nest?"

TACKA-TACKA-TACKA.

"Oh no," groaned Crank, "crabs!"

CLACK-CLACK-CLACK.

"I hates doze crabs," moaned Grunt.

"Yes," said Gore, showing them one of his arms which had been fitted with a sharp metal claw instead of a hand. "They *can* be quite nasty. But they do have their uses and they *really* like the taste of robot.

"SPRINGER!" yelled Gore. "Are you sure we're close enough?"

"Of course," said the little robot, stepping out on to the plank and peering over the edge. "I'm right above the nest now."

"Very good," said Gore, and stamped on the end of the plank. "You're dismissed."

Beneath Gore's heavy foot, the wooden plank rattled and shook, sending Springer toppling over the edge and down into the crabs' nest.

There was a high-pitched squeal as the little robot fell, then a loud CLACK-CLACK, followed by the crunch and squeak of metal being torn apart.

"The captain had grown tired of Springer," explained Gore, "and he really wasn't happy to hear about him beating his poor little botweiler with that metal bar."

Some of the robot pirates grumbled at this but they knew better than to complain out loud.

"The captain's also decided *you'll* be no use in the engine room," said Gore, looking at Al. "So I have to let you go."

"Let me go?" said Al. "But what about the others?"

"I'm sure they don't want to go where *you're* going," said Gore.

With that, Buzzsaw pushed Al on to the wooden plank.

Al staggered forwards along the plank, nearly falling off the end. Looking down he could see straight into the crabs' nest. Hordes of giant crabs were crawling over each other, their deadly pincers reaching hungrily into the air.

"GORE! NO!" cried Avatar, struggling to get free from the ropes that tied the three friends to the mast. "You can't—"

"You're wrong, Avatar," said Gore. "I think you will find that I can."

The big robot stamped on the end of the plank, making it bounce wildly.

For a moment, Al held on tightly as the plank rattled and shook beneath him, but then he lost his grip. Al's hands slipped from the end of the plank and he fell down toward the waiting claws.

Crank, Avatar and Grunt watched in horror as their friend disappeared from view over the side of the ship. There was a short scream and then CLACK-CLACK-CLACK ...

Al was gone.

Falling through the air, Al jabbed frantically at the controls of the anti-grav belt that was fastened round his waist. The ground rushed towards him and the crabs' deadly claws snapped together hungrily.

One of the crabs almost snatched him from the air. Al felt its claw scrape against his arm as it snapped together. Luckily, the crabs were pushing and shoving each other as they tried to grab him, making it harder for each of them. Two sets of claws clashed together and Al dropped between a couple of the giant creatures and landed on the back of another.

Next to him, on the crab's armoured back, lay an arm that Al recognised straight away. It had belonged to Springer, the little robot pirate that had fallen down before him.

Al hadn't liked Springer, but seeing his arm lying there almost made him feel sorry for the old robot.

Staring at the severed arm, Al forgot about the anti-grav belt for a moment, but soon remembered it as another huge claw made a grab for him. Al pushed himself backwards along the top of the crab and turned the dial on the anti-grav belt as far as it would go.

The belt shuddered around his waist but still didn't get Al moving.

Another of the creatures had spotted him sitting on the crab's back and started clambering over the others as it scuttled towards him with its huge pincers snapping at the air.

TACKA-TACKA-TACKA, CLACK-CLACK.

As the deadly pincers reached out, ready to snatch Al from the back of the crab, he jabbed again at the buttons on the anti-grav belt. This time the belt gave a loud whine and Al shot into the air just as the claws snapped together.

Al flew up between the crabs and out above the nest where claws reached and grabbed for him, snapping and clicking in the air. Giving the belt's dial another twist, Al soon had it under control and he hovered at the side of the *Narwhal*, just beneath the plank that was still sticking out from the deck.

With a rumbling sound the ship's huge wooden wheels started to move. The plank above his head was pulled in and the *Narwhal* was on its way once more, rolling across the sun-baked bed of the Ghost Sea with his friends held prisoner on board.

As the great ship went past, Al kept his eyes open for another way to get on board. There were no windows or doors along the sides of the ship, only bare wood, and Al had to wait until it had almost rolled past before finally spotting a way in.

Along the back of the *Narwhal* was a small balcony and a long row of windows. Al grabbed the rail that ran along its edge and pulled himself on to the narrow balcony, then peered in through the windows.

The glass was thick with grime and all Al could make out were shadows in the darkness within. One of the windows was missing completely and, after a quick look to make sure no one was around, he squeezed himself through and into the room beyond.

Once inside, Al switched off the anti-grav belt and looked around. The room was dark and dusty. In the middle stood a large table, heaped with plates, maps and other junk. The walls were decorated with tattered rags but Al guessed they had once been fine cloth that had rotted over the years. Broken pots, jewels and ancient weapons littered the floor and everything smelled old and dusty.

Then Al saw him sitting there.

Partly hidden by the shadows and wall hangings in the corner of the room, a figure sat watching him from its chair.

A fancy-looking hat sat on the figure's head and long hair fell in tatty curls on to the shoulders of its coat. The thin, bony fingers of one hand, decorated with jewelled rings, gripped the arm of the chair. The other hand held the handle of a sword that lay across a small table by its side.

Al froze, hardly daring to move.

"Oh!" he said. "I am sorry to disturb you, captain sir, but I was looking for the engine room and seem to have stumbled in here by mistake."

The figure didn't say a word. It just sat and stared at Al without moving a muscle.

He's probably deciding whether to throw me to the crabs or just cut me in half right now, thought Al miserably.

But still the captain didn't move. He didn't even twitch one of his bony fingers.

It was then Al noticed something strange about the captain. His bony fingers really were bony. *Very* bony ... and although Al hadn't met many softies in his life, he felt quite sure that fingers shouldn't be *quite* as bony as that.

Finally daring to step forwards, Al took a closer look at Captain Silas Quench.

The dreaded Silas Quench, captain of the *Narwhal* and its band of loathsome pirates, the meanest, cruellest softie to ever walk the planet, was dead. It looked as though he'd been dead for a very long time.

The dead captain sat slumped in his chair, covered in dust and old cobwebs. His greying skull peered unseeingly from beneath the wide-brimmed hat, and the fingers that gripped the chair arm were nothing more than dried bones.

Al was staring in disbelief at the dead captain when there was a noise behind him. Light from the setting sun poured into the room and Gore stood framed in the doorway, his body casting sinister shadows across the floor.

"The captain won't be happy," said Gore. "But I'll see what he says."

Al stood for a moment, wondering what Gore was talking about, then realised the robot wasn't talking to him at all. He was still looking at the pirates out on deck.

Diving to the floor, Al crawled behind Silas Quench's chair and hoped the big robot hadn't seen him.

There was a *BANG* as the door slammed shut, blocking out the light, and then silence.

Al waited a few moments and was about to pop his head out from behind the chair when footsteps thumped across the cabin floor towards him.

Something heavy banged on to the table in the middle of the room and there was a crash and clatter as things were swept on to the floor, and Gore's voice boomed out in the darkness.

"NO!" he cried. "YOU CAN'T MAKE THE CREW DO THAT."

There was another crash as something heavy hit the wall. From his hiding place Al saw the remains of a broken stool drop to the floor and wondered what Gore was up to.

Then, as he watched, the big robot walked back to the cabin door and threw it open.

Light flooded back into the room and Al ducked behind the captain's chair again.

"Yes sir, I'll tell them," said Gore, looking back into the room. "It won't happen again."

Then the door closed and Al could hear Gore talking to the robot pirates. There were moans and groans from the crew but Al couldn't hear much of what was being said.

Alone in the dark cabin with the skeleton of Silas Quench, Al sat and thought for a while …

Then he had an idea.

10

Only the ghost of a breeze blew into the sails, but still the *Narwhal* rumbled across the dried sea bed at full speed. Two robot pirates stood at the wheel, steering the ship by the light of the moon.

"Poor old Gore," said Grubscrew. "Did you hear that noise in the captain's cabin?"

"I don't know," grumbled Buzzsaw. "*Something's* not right. How come no one ever sees the captain any more?"

"Don't let Gore hear you talking like that," said Grubscrew. "You saw what happened to poor old Springer."

"Yeah, I saw it," said Buzzsaw. "The old captain never used to do things like that. It's all changed since Gore arrived and I don't trust him."

A dark shadow fell over the two robots and Grubscrew let go of the wheel in surprise.

"Oh!" he cried. "Gore ... we were just—"

"Talking about me?" suggested Gore. "Yes. I heard. And it's such a pity you don't trust me."

"It wasn't me," squeaked Grubscrew, pointing at Buzzsaw. "It was him."

"Don't you worry," growled Gore, drawing a sword from his belt. "I've got something to stop both of you talking."

The sword hummed in the night air and blue sparks flickered and danced along its blade.

"Oh look!" said Grubscrew, backing away. "He's got an energy-blade. I've not seen one of them for years."

"Very nice," said Buzzsaw, dodging Gore's flickering blade. "A weapon like that could cut you in two in the blink of an eye."

As Grubscrew jumped out of the way, Gore swung the energy-blade but missed and hit the ship's wheel, splitting it in two.

The saw-blade on the end of Buzzsaw's arm roared to life and he blocked Gore's next attack, sending up a shower of sparks where the saw touched Gore's arm.

Gore let out a roar and leaped over the broken wheel, bringing the energy-blade down in an arc from behind his head.

Buzzsaw staggered backwards into the wall and there was a crash as something hit the deck near his feet. The robot looked down in surprise to find his arm lying there with the saw-blade still spinning.

Gore was bringing the energy-blade round for a second attack when the cabin door opened in front of him.

"Oh!" said Grubscrew, looking at the figure in the dark doorway. "Captain Quench."

Gore froze to the spot with the energy-blade still held over his head. *"Quench?"* he said, staring into the shadows in disbelief.

"Captain Quench," said Buzzsaw.

"Impossible!" cried Gore. "He's dead."

"Dead?" said Grubscrew and Buzzsaw. "What do you mean he's dead?"

There was a sudden commotion behind the three robots as the rest of the crew came on to the deck to see what the noise was about.

"Well ... he's ... I ..." stammered Gore, letting the energy-blade fall to his side.

The figure in the doorway stepped forwards on to the moonlit deck and pointed at Gore.

"You killed me, Gore," said Quench in a strangely muffled voice.

The pirates gasped on hearing this, but none of them moved. There was something strange about Silas Quench that they couldn't quite put their finger on until Grubscrew spotted it.

"He's got no legs," cried Grubscrew.

As Silas Quench floated across the deck towards the robots, his head tilted slightly and the moonlight fell across his face to reveal a grinning skull beneath the fancy captain's hat.

"Aarghhhh!" screamed one of the pirates. "The captain's a ghost."

Quench's arm reached out once more and pointed accusingly at Gore. "You betrayed me, Gore," said the captain. "Let the prisoners go." Gore was about to run from the ghostly figure when something caught his eye. He'd seen the captain's dried, bony hands many times before but the one pointing at him now didn't look quite right. In fact, it looked metal.

"YOU!" cried Gore, his eyes flashing brightly in the night.

The big robot raised the energy-blade and charged across the deck towards the captain.

Silas Quench dodged quickly to one side and his head fell from his shoulders and rolled across the deck.

"On no you don't," said Grubscrew, sticking his leg out and tripping Gore as he ran past. "You're not killing the captain again."

As the big robot fell to the floor the rest of the pirates charged at him, yelling and waving their weapons.

Gore was on his feet in no time, the energy-blade flickering in his hands.

As the sound of clashing swords filled the air, no one noticed the headless figure of Captain Quench float across the deck and down to the engine room.

*

Crank, Avatar and Grunt were pedalling as fast as they could when the headless figure floated into the engine room.

"I said deze pirates was strange," said Grunt. "Look at dis one."

"I have come to rescue you," said the figure in a muffled voice.

"If you take that ridiculous coat off we might be able to tell what you are saying," said Avatar.

"Oh ... sorry," said the figure and pulled at the buttons on the front of the coat, dropping it to the floor.

"AL!" cried the three friends. "We thought you were—"

"Crushed? Eaten?" suggested Al. "It will take more than a few crabs to finish me."

"What about Gore and the pirates?" said Crank.

"Do not worry about them," said Al. "They are busy."

"Well what is we waitin' for den," said Grunt,

heading for the stairs. "Let's go."

The four friends had hardly taken a step forwards when there was a deafening crash and they were thrown across the floor.

"Who's steering this thing?" cried Crank, as the *Narwhal's* hull tore open in front of them. Chunks of wood and splinters the size of spears flew through the air and the ship tipped to one side, throwing the friends against the wall.

"Look!" said Grunt, when the ship had stopped moving. "I've found a new door."

A huge hole had appeared in the side of the ship, and through it the friends could see the dried mud of the sea bed.

"Come on," said Avatar, leading the way.

The *Narwhal* had hit a huge rock in the sea bed, tearing a hole in its side. One of the masts had split in two and the top half lay in front of them on the dried mud. Something lay crushed beneath it, but the friends couldn't quite tell what it was.

Then Grunt let out a cry and ran forwards.
"Scamp!"

The body of a botweiler lay crushed beneath
the broken mast and Grunt knelt down to
examine it.

Smoke was coming from the
robo-dog's head and its
eyes glowed
dimly in the
dark.

"It's all right," said Grunt. "It's not Scamp. It's only one of Gore's old tin cans."

Then a growl made him look round.

Standing next to Grunt was Gore's other botweiler. Its mouth opened, revealing rusty teeth, and its claws dug into the ground.

Grunt was about to dive out of the way when the robo-dog attacked. It let out a loud snarl and pounced with its deadly jaws wide open.

A terrible crunch and squeal of metal being torn apart filled the air and Grunt let out a loud cry.

"*Good boy*, Scamp," he said. "Just in time."

The big botweiler shook its head, stepped off the remains of the old robo-dog and followed Grunt and the others across the dried sea bed.

"What about Gore?" said Crank, looking back over his shoulder to where the glow of Gore's energy-blade could be seen flickering in the darkness.

"I don't think he's going to be bothering us for a while," said Avatar. "He seems to have his hands full."

In front of them, the three friends could just see the shadowy outline of a great wall rising above the sea bed.

"The ancient walled city of Tarka," said Avatar.

"Do you think we will find Robotika there?" asked Al.

"I don't know," said Avatar. "But I hear there's enough gold hidden there to buy a new starship."

The End

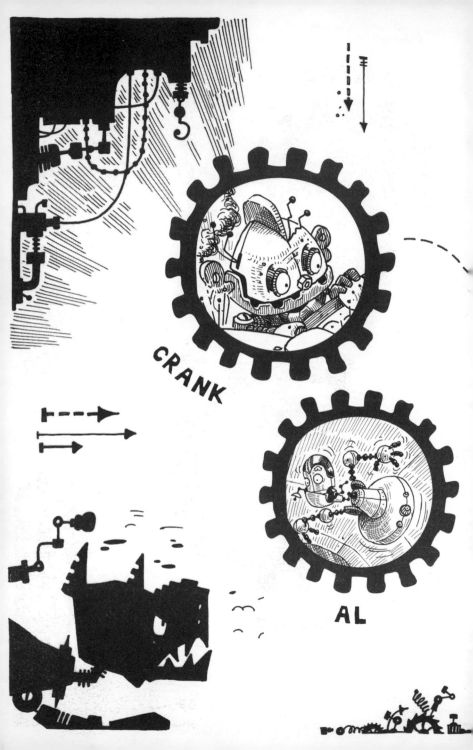

CRANK

AL

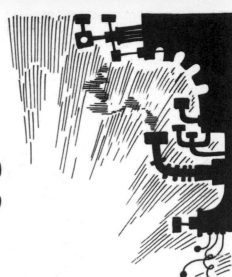

AVATAR

GRUNT

book 6

Aquanauts

Al felt the walkway shake beneath him as another ball of fire hit it, then there was a loud whine from the Dragonfly behind him.

From where they stood, Avatar, Crank and Grunt saw the Dragonfly's wings hit the surface of the water, making it twist to one side, and they watched as the Crodilus tried desperately to keep the flying machine under control. But it was no use.

The Dragonfly flipped over and crashed into the walkway. The columns that supported it toppled into each other like dominoes and collapsed, crushing the Dragonfly and dragging it down beneath the water with them.

Al was running as fast as he could but the walkway was collapsing beneath him and there was nothing Crank, Avatar or Grunt could do apart from watch as their friend dropped into the murky water below.

DAMIAN HARVEY

lives in Blackpool with his wife and three daughters, their four cats, a horde of guinea pigs, a tank full of fish and a quirky imagination.

He loves music, movies, reading, swimming, walking, cheese and ice cream — but not always at the same time.

Before realising how much fun he could have writing and making things up he worked as a lifeguard, had a job in a boring office and once saved the galaxy from invading vampire robots (though none of these were as exciting as they sound).

Damian now spends lots of time in front of his computer but loves getting out to visit schools and libraries to share stories, talk about writing and get people excited about books.